This igloo book
belongs to:

....

igloobooks

Published in 2019
by Igloo Books Ltd
Cottage Farm
Sywell
NN6 0BJ
www.igloobooks.com

Written by Stephanie Moss
Illustrated by Mark Jones

Designed by Nicholas Gage
Edited by Hannah Cather

0719 002.01
4 6 8 10 11 9 7 5
ISBN 978-1-78670-300-2

Printed and manufactured in China

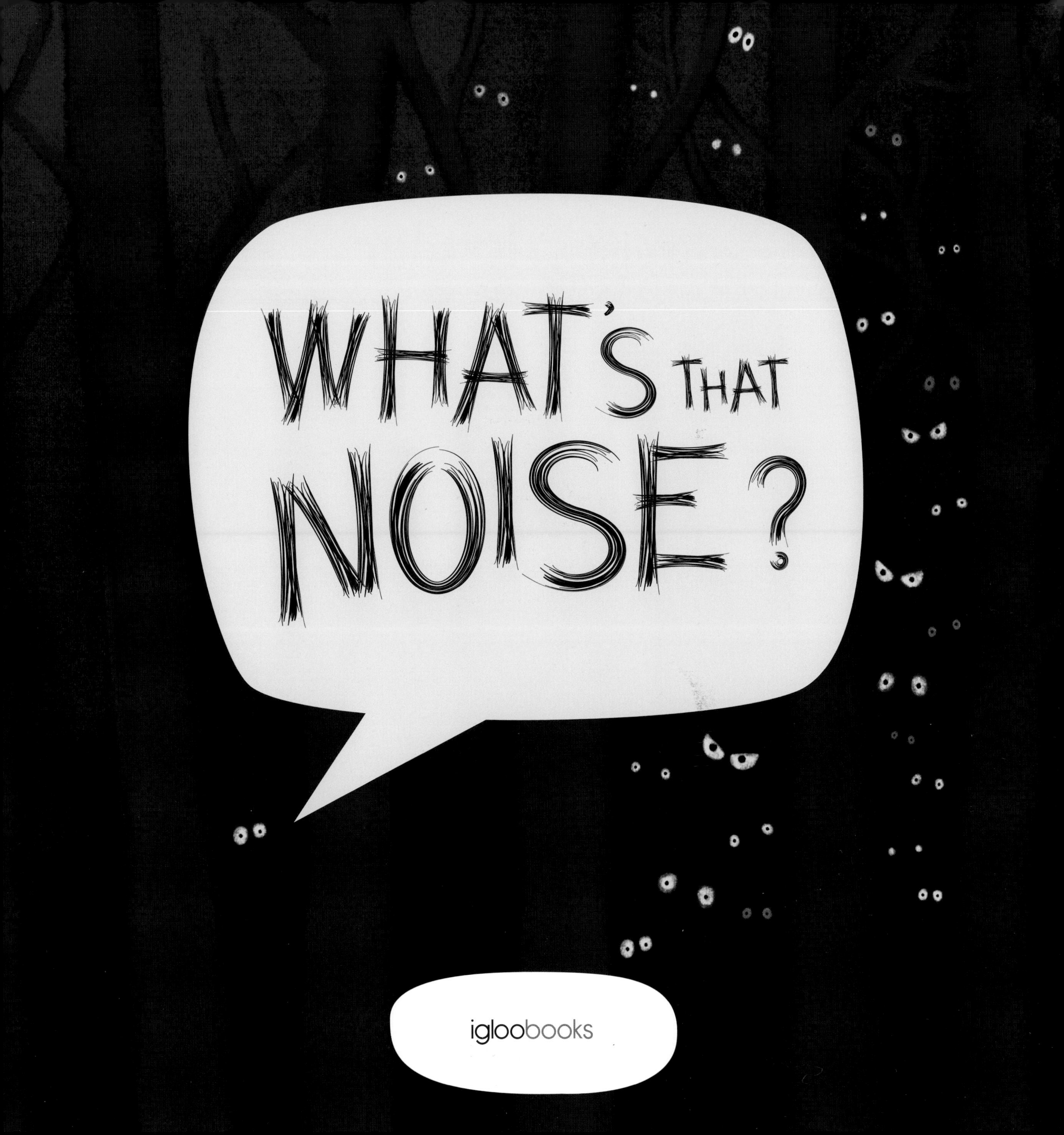
WHAT'S THAT NOISE?
igloobooks

One dark, summer's night, there was
a strange, low, rumbling sort of a roar.

It grew **louder** and **louder** and **louder**...
and then it rumbled again some more.

WHAT'S THAT NOISE?

cried Baby Bunny,
feeling nothing but dread and fright.

Though what crossed Baby Badger's face
was a look of curious delight.

Listen here, this must be it. See, it's not so bad.

Baby Badger pointed to some frogs, each on a lily pad.

As an orchestra

CROAKED,

one frog stopped to say...

... "I wish that **rumbling** would stop. It's been **roaring** all day!"

So they
continued their
search, looking this
way and that,

'til they
stumbled on Fox,
hitting acorns
with a bat!

Suddenly, the real **rumbling** noise was clearer than ever,

so Baby Badger and Baby Bunny both huddled close together.

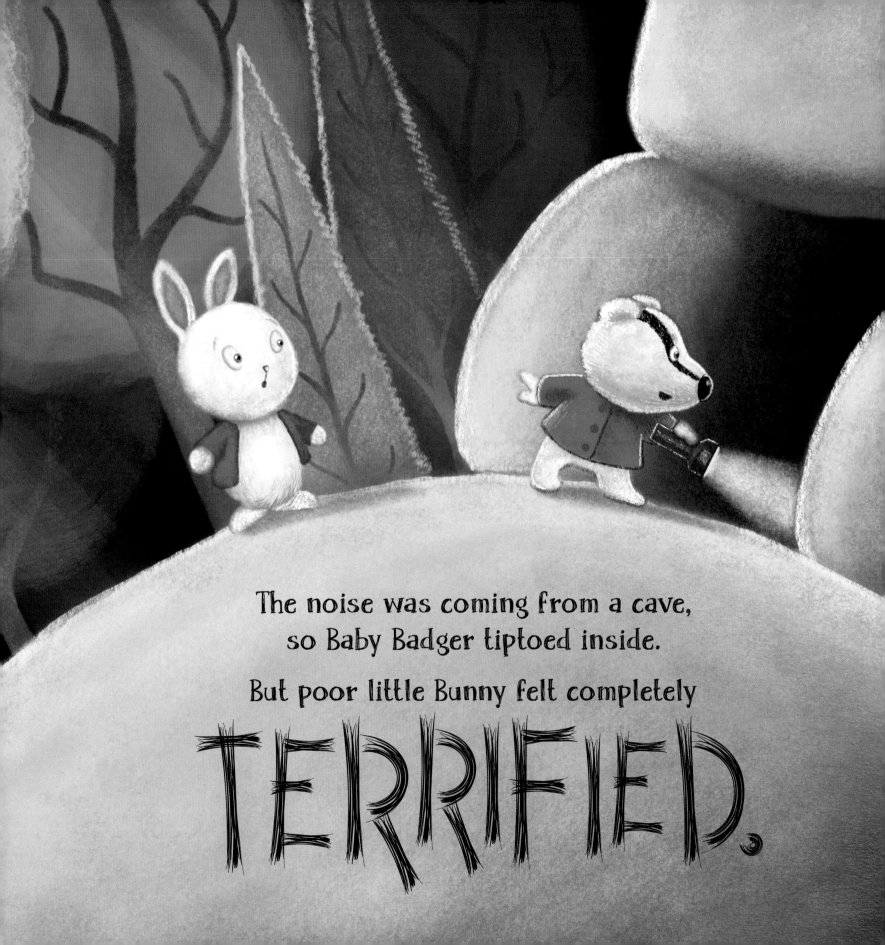

The noise was coming from a cave,
so Baby Badger tiptoed inside.

But poor little Bunny felt completely

TERRIFIED.

Bunny hid behind Badger,
in case they came to any harm.

But when they peered inside,
she saw there was no
cause for alarm.

Baby Bunny said,

It's
Big Bear!

The noise was
him all along.

"A bit of snoring isn't scary.

How could I have been so wrong?"

So they **banged** on pots and pans.

They even **bounced** up on the bed.

It took a while, but Big Bear soon woke up and rubbed his head.

Before everybody knew it,
a forest party was in full swing.

And Baby Bunny learned facing
your fears is more important
than anything.